Blastoff! Readers are carefully developed by literacy experts to build reading stamina and move students toward fluency by combining standards-based content with developmentally appropriate text.

Level 1 provides the most support through repetition of high-frequency words, light text, predictable sentence patterns, and strong visual support.

Level 2 offers early readers a bit more challenge through varied sentences, increased text load, and text-supportive special features.

Level 3 advances early-fluent readers toward fluency through increased text load, less reliance on photos, advancing concepts, longer sentences, and more complex special features.

★ **Blastoff! Universe**

This edition first published in 2023 by Bellwether Media, Inc.

No part of this publication may be reproduced in whole or in part without written permission of the publisher. For information regarding permission, write to Bellwether Media, Inc., Attention: Permissions Department, 6012 Blue Circle Drive, Minnetonka, MN 55343.

Library of Congress Cataloging-in-Publication Data

Names: Sabelko, Rebecca, author.
Title: France / by Rebecca Sabelko.
Description: Minneapolis, MN : Bellwether Media, Inc., 2023. | Series: Blastoff! Readers : countries of the world | Includes bibliographical references and index. | Audience: Ages 5-8 | Audience: Grades 2-3 | Summary: "Relevant images match informative text in this introduction to France. Intended for students in kindergarten through third grade"– Provided by publisher.
Identifiers: LCCN 2022018221 (print) | LCCN 2022018222 (ebook) | ISBN 9781644877180 (library binding) | ISBN 9781648347641 (ebook)
Subjects: LCSH: France–Juvenile literature.
Classification: LCC DC17 .S23 2023 (print) | LCC DC17 (ebook) | DDC 944–dc23/eng/20220427
LC record available at https://lccn.loc.gov/2022018221
LC ebook record available at https://lccn.loc.gov/2022018222

Text copyright © 2023 by Bellwether Media, Inc. BLASTOFF! READERS and associated logos are trademarks and/or registered trademarks of Bellwether Media, Inc.

Editor: Rachael Barnes   Designer: Gabriel Hilger

Printed in the United States of America, North Mankato, MN.

Table of Contents

All About France	4
Land and Animals	6
Life in France	12
France Facts	20
Glossary	22
To Learn More	23
Index	24

All About France

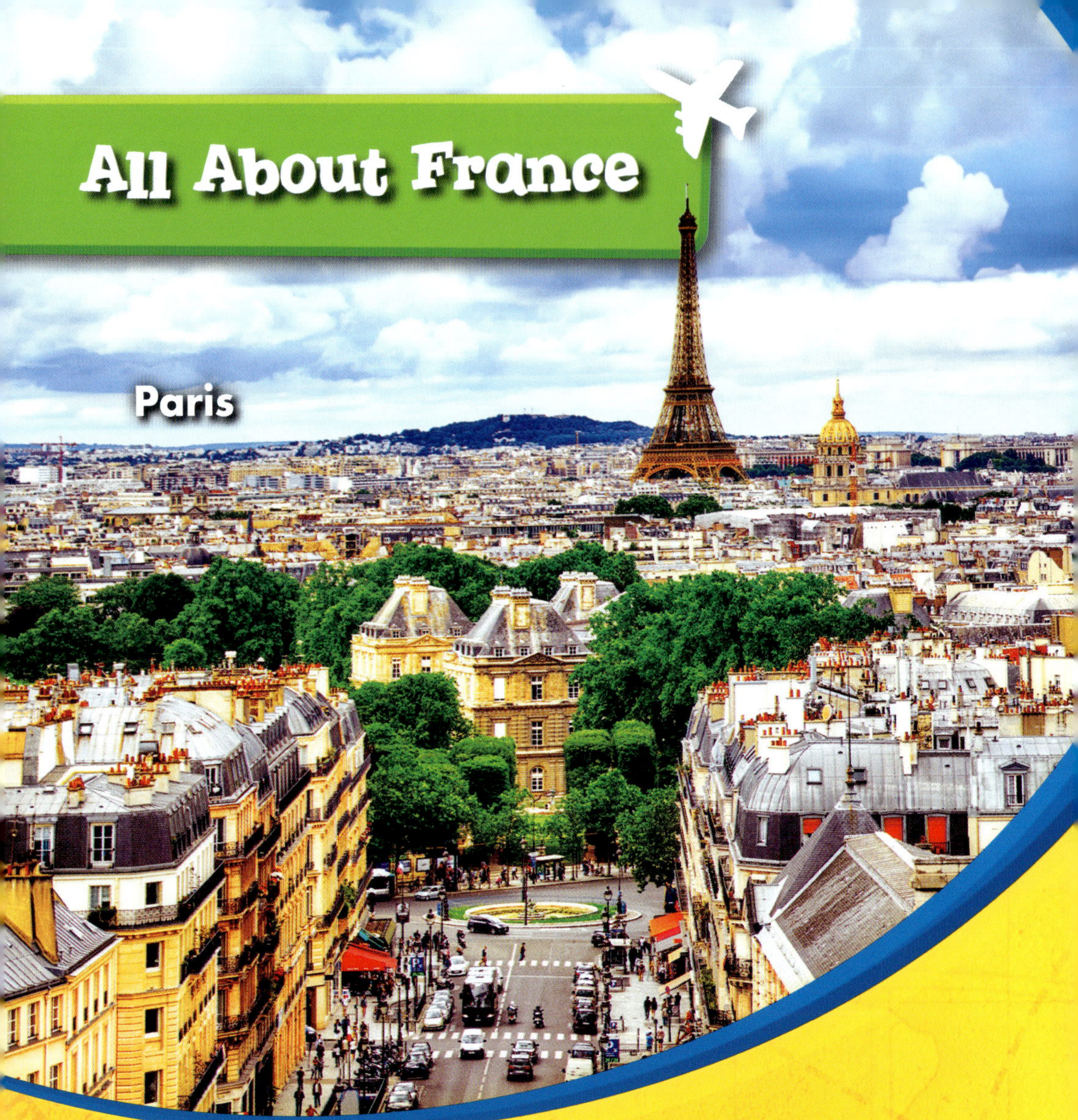

Paris

France is a country in western Europe. It is known for its art.

Paris is France's capital. It is one of the world's most popular cities!

Land and Animals

Plains cover northern France. Low mountains sit in the center. The Loire River runs through them.

The Pyrenees Mountains line southern France. The Alps **range** towers in the southeast.

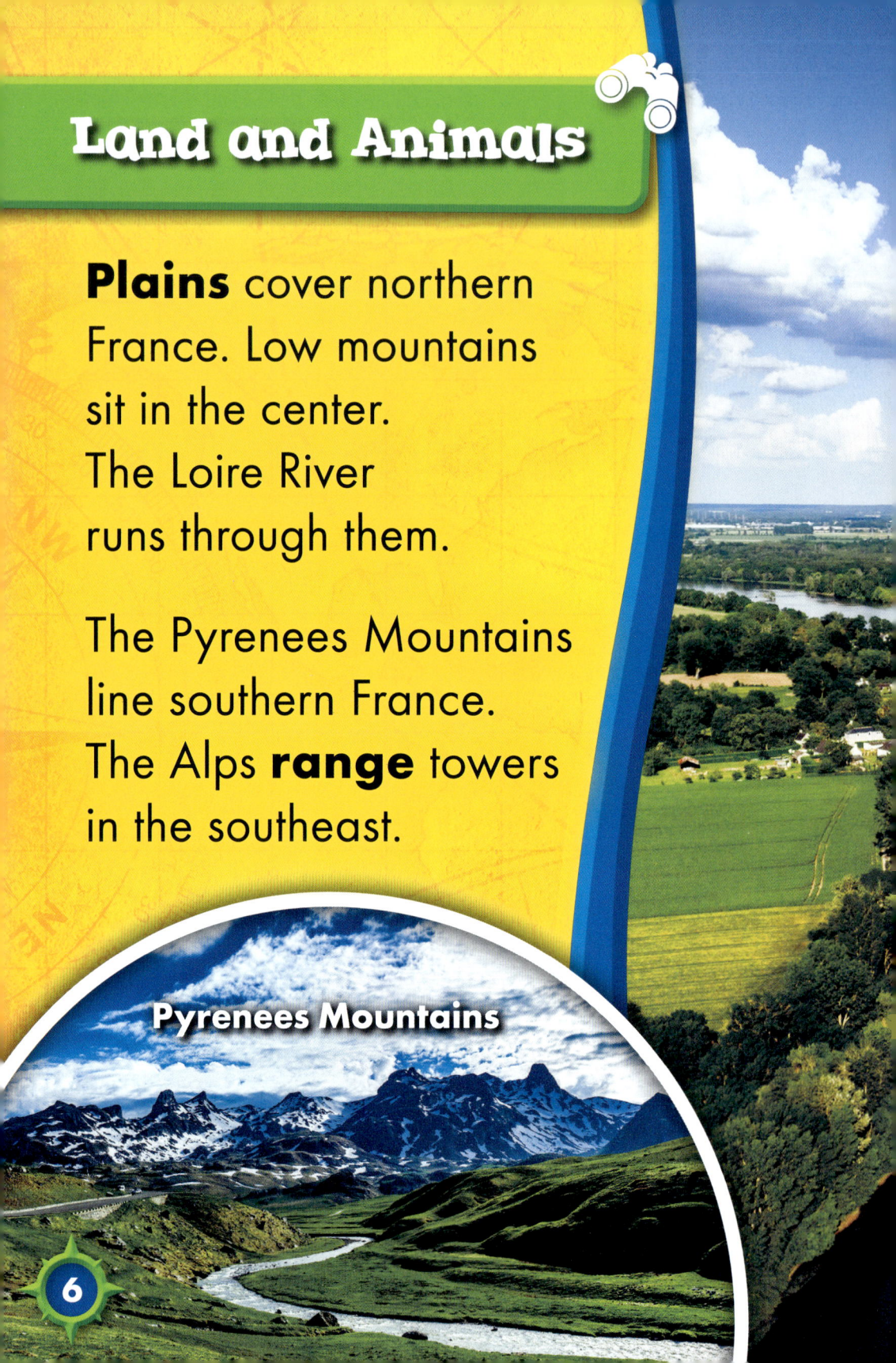

Pyrenees Mountains

Loire River

Size: 634 miles (1,020 kilometers) long
Famous For: France's longest river

Rain and mild weather are common along the coasts. Inland, summers are hot and winters are cold.

Snow covers the southern mountains each winter.

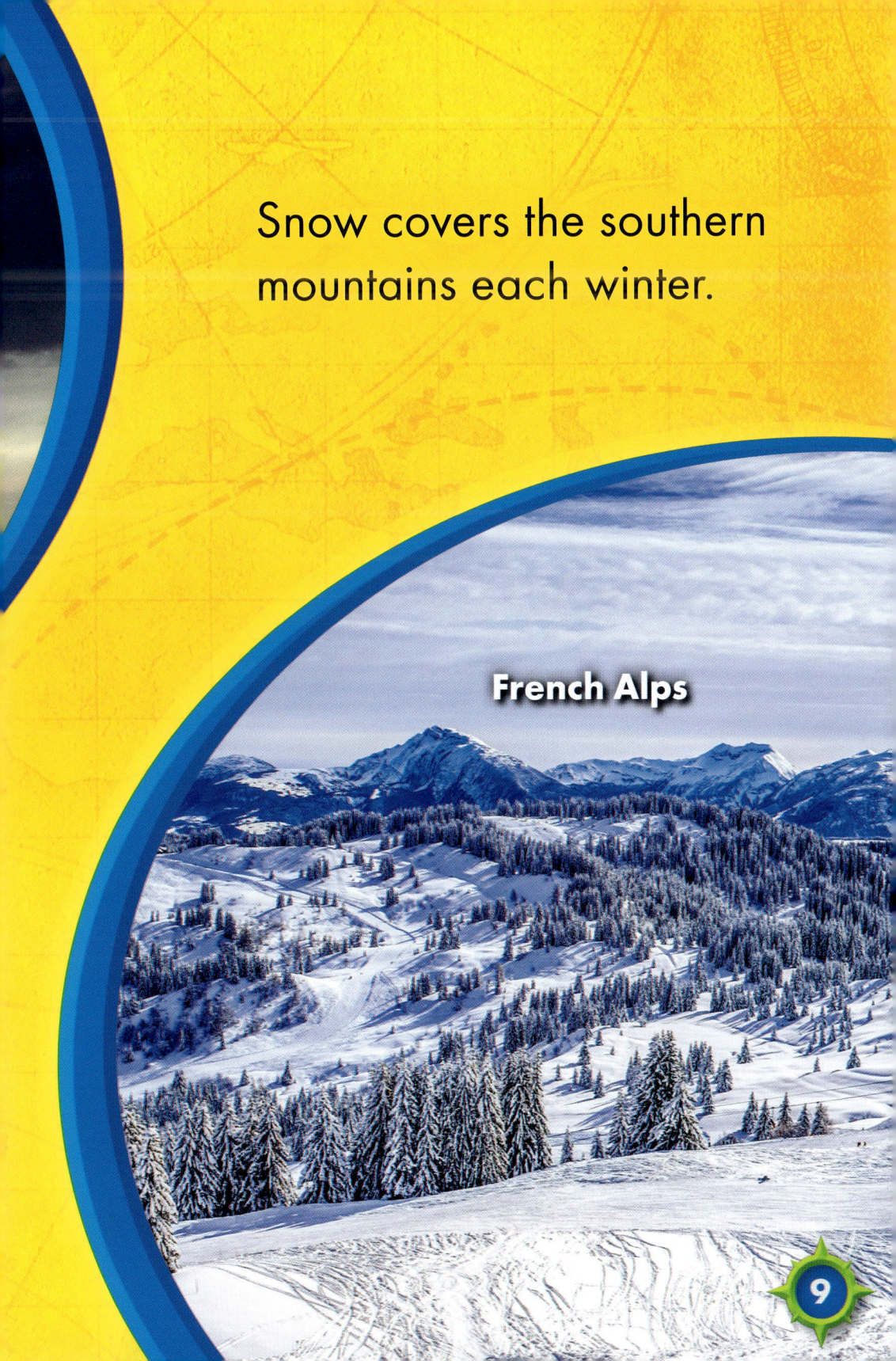

French Alps

Deer run through forests and **meadows**. Genets search for **rodents** to eat.

Animals of France

red deer

genet

green lizard

Egyptian vulture

Green lizards catch **insects** in tall grasses. Vultures stop in France as they **migrate**.

Life in France

Many people **settled** in France throughout history. **Immigrants** continue to call the country home.

French is spoken throughout the nation. Many people are **Christians**.

Notre-Dame Church

Tour de France

soccer

Many people enjoy cycling. Bicyclists race each year in the Tour de France. Soccer is another popular sport.

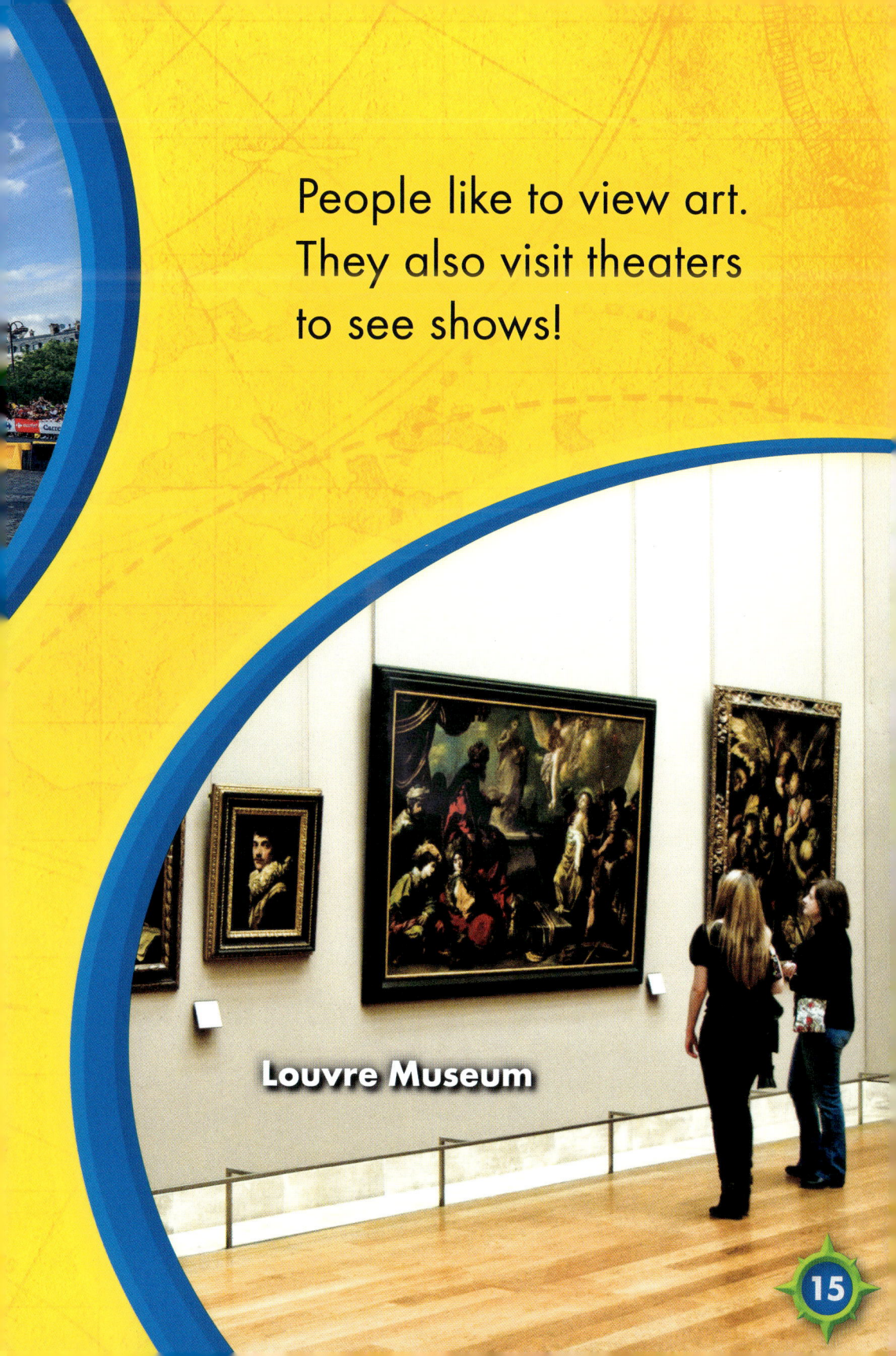

People like to view art. They also visit theaters to see shows!

Louvre Museum

Croissants are soft breakfast rolls. Thin pancakes called *crêpes* are common treats.

French Foods

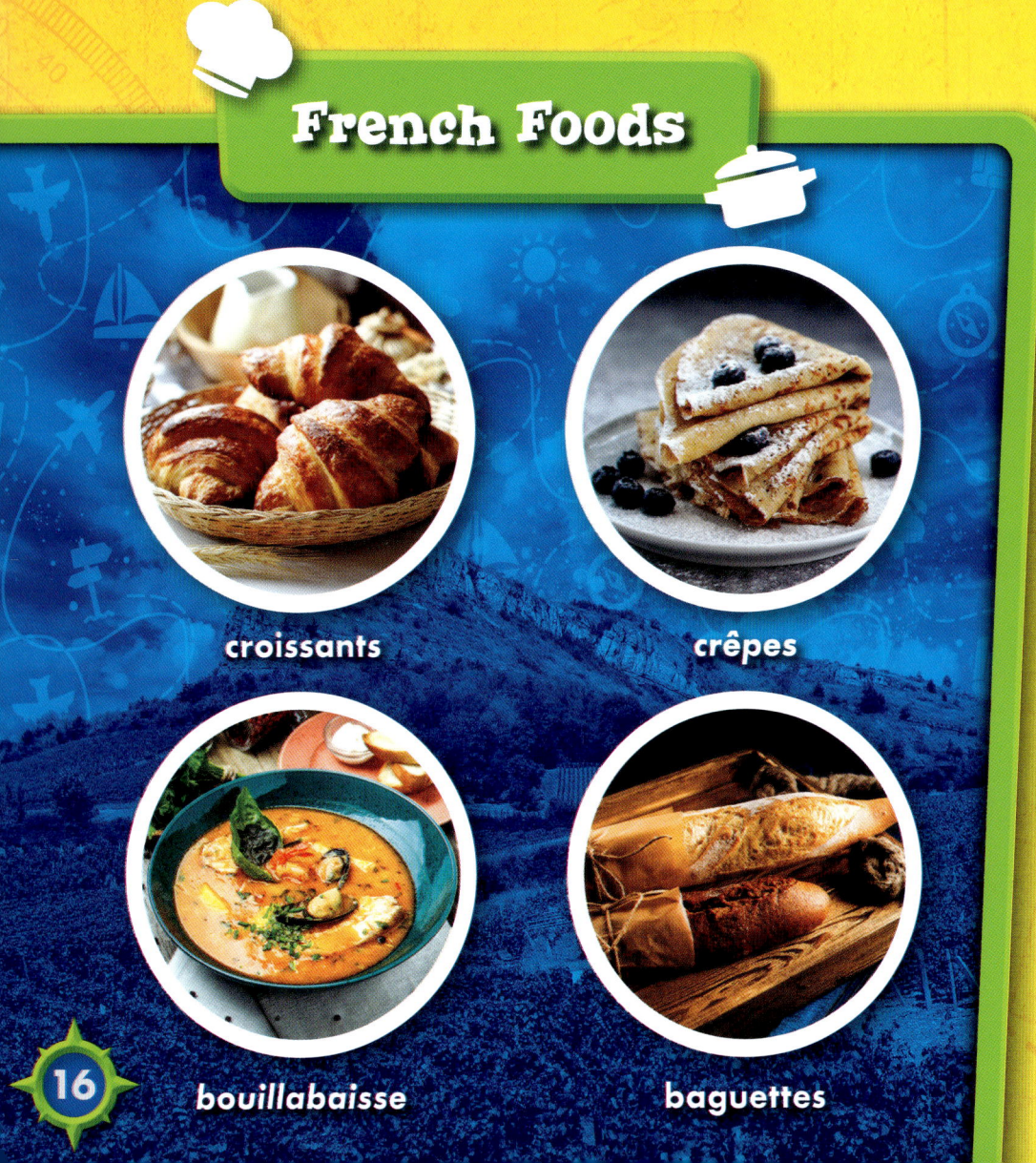

croissants

crêpes

bouillabaisse

baguettes

baguettes

A favorite fish soup is *bouillabaisse*. Cheese and baguettes are **staples**.

February 2 is Candlemas. Christians light candles and eat crêpes.

Bastille Day

Bastille Day is July 14. A parade in Paris honors the French **Republic**. Holidays bring the French together!

France Facts

Size:
212,935 square miles
(551,500 square kilometers)

Population:
68,305,148 (2022)

National Holiday:
Bastille Day (July 14)

Main Language:
French

Capital City:
Paris

Famous Face

Name: Clarisse Agbegnenou

Famous For: an Olympic gold and silver medal winner in judo

Religions

- Muslim: 4%
- other: 13%
- Christian: 50%
- none: 33%

Top Landmarks

Eiffel Tower

Etretat Cliffs

Louvre Museum

Glossary

Christians—people who believe in the words of Jesus Christ

immigrants—people who move to a new country

insects—small animals with six legs and hard outer bodies; an insect's body is divided into three parts.

meadows—lands that are covered, or mostly covered, with grass

migrate—to move from one place to another, often with the seasons

plains—large areas of flat land

range—a group of mountains

republic—a government in which people choose the leader through voting

rodents—small animals that gnaw on their food; mice, rats, and squirrels are all rodents.

settled—made a home in a new place

staples—widely used foods or other items

To Learn More

AT THE LIBRARY
Arrhenius, Ingela P. *My First Book of Paris*. Somerville, Mass.: Candlewick Press, 2021.

Dean, Jessica. *France*. Minneapolis, Minn.: Jump!, 2019.

Spanier, Kristine. *Eiffel Tower*. Minneapolis, Minn.: Jump!, 2021.

ON THE WEB

FACTSURFER

Factsurfer.com gives you a safe, fun way to find more information.

1. Go to www.factsurfer.com.
2. Enter "France" into the search box and click 🔍.
3. Select your book cover to see a list of related content.

Index

Alps, 6
animals, 10, 11
art, 4, 15
Bastille Day, 19
Candlemas, 18
capital (see Paris)
Christians, 12, 18
cycling, 14
Europe, 4
foods, 16, 17, 18
France facts, 20–21
French (language), 12, 13
immigrants, 12
Loire River, 6, 7
map, 5

mountains, 6, 9
Paris, 4, 5, 19
people, 12, 14, 15
plains, 6
Pyrenees Mountains, 6
say hello, 13
soccer, 14
summers, 8
Tour de France, 14
weather, 8, 9
winters, 8, 9

The images in this book are reproduced through the courtesy of: Catarina Belova, front cover, p. 21 (Louvre Museum); Vitaly Titov, front cover; LENS-68, pp. 2-3; Diego Barbieri, p. 3; V_E, pp. 4-5; by-studio, p. 6; Florian Fortier, pp. 6-7; Roman Till Kraemer, pp. 8-9; pidjoe, p. 9; Reflex Nature, pp. 10-11, 22-23; mamboo, p. 11 (red deer); Pablo Santana Duran, p. 11 (genet); MLArduengo, p. 11 (green lizard); Jesus Giraldo Gutierrez, p. 11 (Egyptian vulture); saiko3p, p. 12; MNStudio, pp. 12-13; Frederic Legrand - COMEO, pp. 14-15; Influential Photography, p. 14 (inset); Steve Hamblin/ Alamy, p. 15; P-Kheawtasang, p. 16 (croissants); Mycleverway, p. 16 (crêpes); WhiteYura, p. 16 (bouillabaisse); Tetiana Liubarska, p. 16 (baguettes); TsElena, p. 17; Xinhua/ Alamy, pp. 18-19; titoOnz, p. 20 (flag); REUTERS/ Alamy, p. 20 (Clarisse Agbegnenou); Aerial-motion, p. 21 (Eiffel Tower); prosign, p. 21 (Etretat Cliffs).